Here, kitty, kitty!
¡Ven, gatita, ven!

by Pat Mora

Illustrated by Maribel Suárez

rayo *An Imprint of HarperCollinsPublishers*

Our new kitty likes to hide.

A nuestra nueva gatita le gusta esconderse.

She hides under the table.
Se esconde debajo de la mesa.

She hides under the bed.
Se esconde debajo de la cama.

She hides behind the curtains and behind the sofa.
Se esconde detrás de las cortinas y del sofá.

Danny says, "Here, kitty, kitty. Here, kitty, kitty."

Danny dice —¡Ven, gatita, ven!

Kitty hides behind Grandma's shoes.

La gatita se esconde detrás de los zapatos de Abuelita.

She hides under the newspaper
Se esconde bajo el periódico,

and in my closet.
y en mi ropero.

She jumps inside Tina's doll crib.
Brinca dentro de la cunita de muñecas de Tina.

Tina says, "Here, kitty, kitty. Here, kitty, kitty."
Tina dice —¡Ven, gatita, ven!

Kitty jumps inside a flowerpot.
La gatita brinca dentro de una maceta.

I crawl very slowly and very softly.
Yo me acerco, muy despacito y muy calladita.

I say, "Here, kitty, kitty. Here, kitty, kitty."
La llamo —¡Ven, gatita, ven!

I almost touch her,
Casi la toco,

but she runs and hides again.
pero corre y se esconde otra vez.

Then kitty comes close. I pet my soft friend.
Luego se acerca y acaricio a mi amiga dulce.

To Joseph Rodriguez, Patricia Armendariz,
and Sara Howrey, friends and literary champions
—P.M.
A Joseph Rodriguez, Patricia Armendariz y
Sara Howrey, amigos y campeones de la literatura
—P.M.

Rayo is an imprint of HarperCollins Publishers.

Here, Kitty, Kitty! / ¡Ven, gatita, ven!
Text copyright © 2008 by Pat Mora
Illustrations copyright © 2008 by Maribel Suárez
Manufactured in China.
Library of Congress Cataloging-in-Publication Data is available.
ISBN 978-0-06-085044-9 (trade bdg.) — ISBN 978-0-06-085045-6 (lib. bdg.)

Design by Stephanie Bart-Horvath
1 2 3 4 5 6 7 8 9 10
❖
First Edition